FUN FIRST CONCEPTS

LET'S LEARN COLORS

by Anna C. Peterson

TABLE OF CONTENTS

tadpole books

WORDS TO KNOW

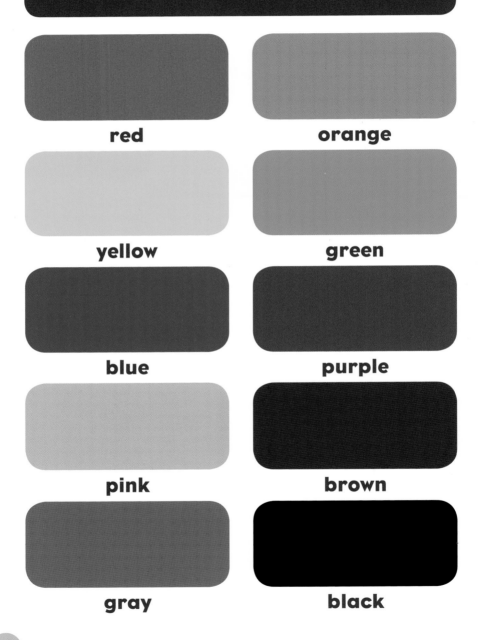

red

orange

yellow

green

blue

purple

pink

brown

gray

black

LET'S LEARN COLORS!

This bug is red.

butterfly

This bug is orange.

This bug is yellow.

This bug is green.

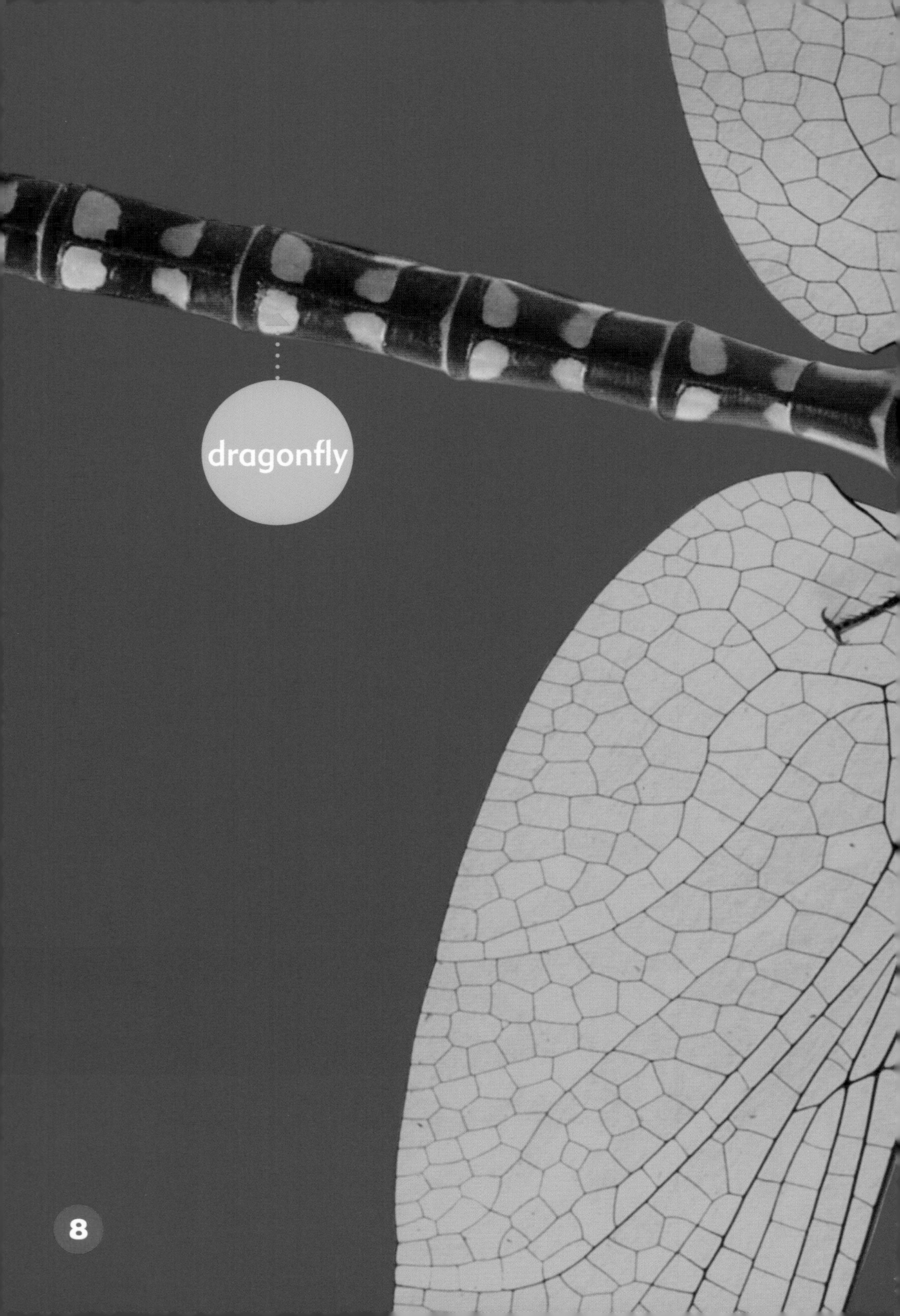
dragonfly

This bug is blue.

This bug is purple.

This bug is pink.

stink bug

This bug is brown.

This bug is gray.

This bug is black.

LET'S REVIEW!

What colors do you see on this bug?

INDEX